INDEX

KU-438-622

Series 413

© LADYBIRD BOOKS LTD MCMLXVI
All rights reserved. No part of this publication may be reproduced, stored in a retrieval system, or transmitted in any form or by any means, electronic, mechanical, photo-copying, recording or otherwise, without the prior consent of the copyright owner.

A SECOND LADYBIRD BOOK OF

Nursery Rhymes

with illustrations
by FRANK HAMPSON

Ladybird Books Loughborough

Mary had a little lamb,
Its fleece was white as snow;
And everywhere that Mary went
The lamb was sure to go.

It followed her to school one day,
That was against the rule;
It made the children laugh and play
To see a lamb at school.

There was an old woman
who lived in a shoe,

She had so many children
she didn't know what to do;

She gave them some broth
without any bread;

Then whipped them all soundly
and sent them to bed.

Tom, Tom, the piper's son,

Stole a pig and away did run;

The pig was eat

And Tom was beat,

And Tom went howling down
the street.

Hot cross buns !

Hot cross buns !

One a penny, two a penny,

Hot cross buns !

If you have no daughters,

Give them to your sons,

One a penny, two a penny,

Hot cross buns !

Lucy Locket lost her pocket,

Kitty Fisher found it;

Not a penny was there in it,

But a ribbon round it.

Old King Cole

Was a merry old soul,

And a merry old soul was he;

He called for his pipe,

And he called for his bowl,

And he called for his fiddlers three.

Hark, hark,

The dogs do bark,

The beggars are coming to town ;

Some in rags,

And some in jags,

And one in a velvet gown.

I had a little nut tree,

    Nothing would it bear

But a silver nutmeg

    And a golden pear.

The King of Spain's daughter

    Came to visit me,

And all for the sake

    Of my little nut tree.

Peter, Peter, pumpkin eater,

Had a wife and couldn't keep her;

He put her in a pumpkin shell

And there he kept her very well.

Pumpkin-Eater

Two little dicky birds

Sat upon a wall;

One named Peter

The other named Paul.

Fly away, Peter!

Fly away, Paul!

Come back, Peter!

Come back, Paul!

Mary, Mary, quite contrary,

How does your garden grow?

With silver bells and cockle shells

And pretty maids all in a row.

The north wind doth blow,

And we shall have snow,

And what will poor robin do then?

Poor thing!

He'll sit in a barn,

And keep himself warm,

And hide his head under his wing.

Poor thing!

Yankee Doodle came to town,

Riding on a pony;

He stuck a feather in his cap

And called it macaroni.

Jack Sprat could eat no fat,

His wife could eat no lean,

And so between them both, you see,

They licked the platter clean.

One, two, three, four, five,

Once I caught a fish alive.

Six, seven, eight, nine, ten,

Then I let it go again.

Why did you let it go?

Because it bit my finger so.

Which finger did it bite?

This little finger on the right.

There was a little girl,
> and she had a little curl,

Right in the middle
> of her forehead ;

When she was good,
> she was very, very good,

But when she was bad,
> she was horrid.

Doctor Foster went to Gloucester

In a shower of rain ;

He stepped in a puddle,

Right up to his middle,

And never went there again.

Pease porridge hot,

Pease porridge cold,

Pease porridge in the pot,

Nine days old.

Some like it hot,

Some like it cold,

Some like it in the pot,

Nine days old.

Jack and Jill went up the hill

    To fetch a pail of water;

Jack fell down and broke his crown,

    And Jill came tumbling after.

Up Jack got, and home did trot,

    As fast as he could caper,

To old Dame Dob, who patched
                his nob

    With vinegar and brown paper.

Little Polly Flinders

Sat among the cinders,

Warming her pretty little toes ;

Her mother came and caught her,

And whipped her little daughter

For spoiling her nice new clothes.

Goosey, goosey gander,

Where shall I wander?

Upstairs and downstairs

And in my lady's chamber.

There I met an old man

Who would not say his prayers,

I took him by the left leg

And threw him down the stairs.

Old Mother Hubbard

Went to the cupboard,

To get her poor dog a bone;

But when she got there

The cupboard was bare

And so the poor dog had none.

Little Boy Blue,

    Come blow your horn,

The sheep's in the meadow,

    The cow's in the corn.

But where is the boy

    Who looks after the sheep?

He's under a haycock,

    Fast asleep.

Will you wake him?

    No, not I,

For if I do,

    He's sure to cry.

What are little boys made of?

Frogs and snails

And puppy-dogs' tails,

That's what little boys are made of.

What are little girls made of?

Sugar and spice

And all that's nice,

That's what little girls are made of.

Series 413